Once
I Ate
a Pie

by Patricia MacLachlan and Emily MacLachlan Charest

illustrated by Katy Schneider

JOANNA COTLER BOOKS
An Imprint of HarperCollins*Publishers*

Library of Congress Cataloging-in-Publication Data

MacLachlan, Patricia.

Once I ate a pie : by Patricia MacLachlan and Emily MacLachlan Charest ; illustrated by Katy Schneider.— 1st ed.

p.   cm.

ISBN-10: 0-06-073531-7 — ISBN-10: 0-06-073532-5 (lib. bdg.)

ISBN-13: 978-0-06-073531-9 — ISBN-13: 978-0-06-073532-6 (lib. bdg.)

1. Dogs—Juvenile poetry. 2. Children's poetry, American. I. MacLachlan, Emily. II. Schneider, Katy. III. Title.

PS3563.A3178O53 2006   2004022225

811'.54—dc22

Typography by Alicia Mikles

1 2 3 4 5 6 7 8 9 10

❖

First Edition

This book is for Jamie MacLachlan and all the dogs who love him.
—P. M., E. M. C.

For Olive, Mae, and Ellis, with love
—K. S.

Puppy

The world is **big**.

Trees too tall.

Sky too HIGH.

Snow over my head.

What if I get lost?

"You will chase snowflakes in winter," the people tell me.
"Run through the grasses in spring
and howl at the full moon."

Not now. I am a puppy.
For now I will stay here
by your side.

Safe.

Warm.

Puppy.

Mr. Beefy

I am not thin, but I am beautiful.

When

no

one

is

looking, I steal tubs of butter off the table.

I take them to the basement to eat in private.

Once I ate a PIE.

Gus

I want my people in a group. Like sheep.

When someone is in the bathroom, I open the door.

"Are you all right?"

They are NOT happy.

I take them back to the others.

When they go anywhere,

I am watching.

I am the herder.

Lucy

I was adopted from a shelter.

I **love** the couch. It is **mine**.

The chairs and beds are **mine**, too.

And the house.

At night I sleep between my owners.

They gave me a pillow of my own.

Mine.

Wupsi

My name is Wupsi, but they call me "cute."

"Who's cute?" they ask, smiling.
I cover my eyes with my paws and *pretend* to sleep.

"Who's cute?" they call again.

I run to them. I can't help it.

I am cute.

Darla

I don't like other dogs.

I like **people** and I like the cat who lives with me.

When I want to go out, I bat the bell that hangs next

to the door.

The people come R U N N I N G.

I bat the bell many times a day.

The people are *very tired.*

When they finally go to bed, I wait.

Then, when they are asleep,

I bat the bell one more time.

Louis

I used to yip.

Now I BARK.

I BARK to wake people up.

I BARK when the doorbell rings.

I BARK when someone walks by the house.

I BARK at the television.

I BARK when I want to eat.

I BARK when I want to sit where you are sitting.

BARK!

BARK!

BARK!

Sugar

I'm T I R E D. I want to stay in bed.

I don't want to go outside.

I don't want to take a walk.

I don't want to go in the car.

I like to sleep.

No, I'm not ready to eat.

No, I don't want a snack.

Put the covers back over my head.

I only get out of bed to chase the cat.

And he's not around.

Is he?

Three

We are three.

We are

RUNNERS.

LEAPERS.

CHASERS.

We are soft.

Sweet.

Shy.

We are kings.

We are queens.

We are friends.

We are three.

Needle Nose

I have a very good nose.

It is sharp and useful.

I use it to get into what I love,

the insides of all things:

the refrigerator

the dishwasher

quilts

pillows

dog-cookie boxes

cat-snack bags

toys—I like the squeaker.

I can open mail, too.

If something is closed, I open it.

If it is perfect, I tear it apart.

I love my work.

I love my nose.

Pocket

They say I am tiny.

I used to sleep in a coat pocket.

I have a tiny collar and a tiny coat for when it rains.

I have a tiny dish to eat my food, and a tiny water bowl.

I don't know why my things are so tiny.

I am HUGE.

Abby

I do not steal.

I borrow.

Other dogs' **bones**

and **stuffed animals**

balls

and pull toys.

My people's slippers

and socks

sweaters

and underpants.

But my favorite things to borrow are kitchen things—

loaves of bread from the counter

meat off a plate

anything in a bowl.

I don't have to give those things back.

Tillie and Maude

We look alike.

I am shy.

I do what they tell me.

I like to eat.

I like to chase balls.

I pick private places to go to the bathroom.

When there is food on the table, I can be trusted.

We look alike.

Except for one thing:

I love Tillie.

But we are not alike.

I am sly.

Sometimes I am bad.

I bury my food under the couch cushions.

I like to sleep.

I don't care where I do it. Yesterday I did it in the living room.

Not me.

But we are different.

I love Maude.

Luke

The sun is warm

And I sleep.

I dream about when I was young.

I chased snowflakes in winter.

And ran through the grasses in spring.

I still bark when I want to.

And tonight I might howl at the moon.

But now the sun is warm.

And I sleep.

And dream.